CASH, CARS & COLLEGE

A YOUNG PERSON'S GUIDE TO MONEY.

JANINE BOLON

Cash,
Cars
&
College

A Young Person's Guide to Money

Janine Bolon

The stories and anecdotes described in this book are based on personal experiences of the author and her clients. Most of the names are pseudonyms, and some situations have been modified slightly for educational purposes and to protect the individuals' privacy. This book is not designed to provide specific legal, investment, or accounting advice or any professional service by its publication. Each individual's situation is unique, so specific financial questions should be addressed to a suitable professional. The Author and Publisher specifically disclaim any liability that is incurred from the use or application of the contents of this book.

Visit our website at www.smartcentsinc.com

Cover Design and Illustrations by David Glenn

Published by SmartCents, Inc.

First edition published 2006

ISBN 978-0-6151-3730-8

To my children,

Sean, Beth, Jim, and Clare,

in the hope that they may benefit
from my own hard-won experiences
without the need to travel
the dark road of fiscal trials
all by themselves.

Fly high, fly far.

Acknowledgements

This book would have been impossible to write had it not been for the willingness of all my students to share their innermost financial lives. Thank you for telling me everything that you were doing to make, save, and spend money. You kept me going during the dark days of writer's block by e-mailing me often, demanding copies of the book, as well as reminding me that I had *promise*d to write it for you! I appreciate all the hassling you gave me – and the patience.

Thank you, Kelly Rogers. Your total confidence that I could hold the attention of 12-year-olds for six hours kept me from fleeing in fear from that first youth seminar.

Thank you, Ruth Hailstone. You listened to all my vent sessions as each phase of this book was written and rewritten. I really think we need to throw a whine and cheese party!

David Glenn, you rock when it comes to the graphics, my man. You make this book look SO good!

Heather Fife, if you hadn't watched over my four kids, this book would have never met the publishing deadline. Thank you for child wrangling while I hid in my office, ignored the chaos of everyday life, and wrote.

Last (but not least), to my wonderful mate, Brad, thanks for all of the support, praise, encouragement, and editing. Your painstaking efforts made this book all the better. I'm thrilled that you are in my life.

Contents

I Need Money!

I still remember the day my world changed forever.

I was ten years old, standing alone in an open field looking at the bright blue sky. My dad was stationed at a naval base on the Caribbean island of Eleuthera in the Bahamas. (Yeah, go ahead and envy me; the Bahamas are a really, really cool place to spend your childhood!) A hawk was circling above me. I marveled at how this large bird was held high aloft, seemingly without effort, as it rode a thermal originating from the beach cliff below. As I gazed at it hovering over the beach in its search for prey, I envied its ability to fly. I tried to imagine what it would be like to be looking down in lonely splendor from such an exalted height.

Suddenly, BAM! Out of nowhere a random thought popped into my head: "*I need money!*" This notion was so radical for my young brain that I remember feeling like I was falling. It took a moment for me to regain my balance and grasp the true significance of this strange new concept. I realized that I would never be as independent and free as the soaring hawk above me until I was making and using money to care for myself. In that single instant, I grew up.

You see, my parents did not believe in giving their children an allowance. My dad was particularly fond of saying, "Kid, all we owe you is a place to live, food to keep you alive, and clothing to keep you warm. If you don't like what you get, then go get your own money." To some of you this may seem like a harsh way to grow up, especially when the message was first delivered at the tender age of eight years. It wasn't. My dad did not throw me to the wolves of the world without a sturdy education. He spent the next ten years teaching me how to identify money-making opportunities and then turn them into winning businesses. My dad was a champion at finding potentially profitable prospects anywhere and everywhere; to him there were no limits to what a person could do or how much one could earn. Many evenings at the dinner table he would school me on the fine art of making more money and having more time for fun by the simple choice of being self-employed. Any time I became discouraged or wanted to give up on a project, he would tell me, "Kid, the world doesn't owe you one dime. If you need money, then put on your thinking cap and create a way to help someone so they'll pay you for the service."

I'm lucky that I have adopted his attitude about money in life. You are equally lucky that this book will show you now, in your teen years, the financial principles I learned at 10, 18, 27, and 33 years of age. At each life stage I discovered a new rule of wealth accumulation, through my own experiences, that eventually lead to my family's true financial independence before I had even turned 40. Sure, my husband had a great job that paid well, but it also took careful savings and knowing what we wanted out of life to take a good income and turn it into true wealth. Jump for joy that you are learning these lessons now. Why? Because you will be able to use all my family's years of accumulated financial knowledge to get a major head start on your own path to financial independence.

I have frequently been told that if I was going to succeed in teaching these principles to young people then I would need to change my personal style to better meet your specific needs. Forgive me, but I disagree. I'm going to write to you as if I were speaking to a friend, just as I would to anyone of any age who comes to me for financial advice. Why? Because you can handle it. This information is in no way dumbed down or simplified into platitudes just because you are "kids." I know all too well how irritating a lecture from a condescending adult can be. Besides, you're smarter than that, and *we both know it*.

Do not be fooled by this little book. It is packed with over thirty years of personal experience and ten years of data generated during my fiscal seminars that have proven beyond doubt that this system works. It does not matter how much money you make or what state your current finances are in. *Use the simple techniques in this book and you will eventually grow to be debt-free and financially independent.*

Throughout this book you will see exercises and "to do" items that will require you to think and to write. It is a natural response to quickly answer the questions in your head and never write them down. *Don't take this short cut.* If you do not finish all the exercises just as they are stated, then your results will be so unclear in your mind that you'll either become racked with indecision and do nothing at all to make your hard-earned money grow or else throw down the book in disgust because you think, "Mrs. Bolon doesn't know what she's talking about! This stuff doesn't work!"

But you would be wrong. This system does work, and it works really, really well. I have dozens of students just your age (between 12 to 19 years old) who have used these principles with success – including myself. The point here is to avoid the enticing lure of so-called short cuts. I've tried "quicker paths" and "sure deals" and "easy roads" in my attempts to make more money and gain my independence, and so have my clients. I have learned by hard experience which of these tricks will work and which ones won't. I can also call upon two decades of personal experience as an adult as well as the insights learned by hundreds of adult clients (ages 22 to 78) who have shared their own financial successes and failures with me. Trust me! *I do know what I'm talking* about when it comes to finding the safe and sure highway to financial happiness.

This book has been in the making for a long time. It all started with the first financial seminar I gave for adults in Utah during 2004. At the time I was providing financial mentoring to 33 families as a part of my thesis research for a Master's degree in Education. After I published my thesis in book form (as *Money ... It's Not Just for Rich People!* [Lulu, 2005]), many parents began haranguing me to write a financial book for kids so that they could help their own children learn the same principles of wealth accumulation and financial independence from an early age.

I was hesitant to undertake such a project since my own focus was on adult financial education and I had never taught young people before. The thought of trying to capture and sustain the attention of a group of 12-year-olds was quite daunting. However, after much persuasion and the continuous assurances of a very stubborn friend (thank you, Kelly Rogers!), I reworked my system for a younger audience and held a seminar to test these principles with the help of an eager group of 22 young adult volunteers. Some of the participants wanted to start their own businesses, some were enrolled in college, others already had debt and wanted help digging out of their financial holes. All of the stories in this book are true, although names have been changed to protect privacy. All 22 participants in this study saw an increase in their savings as well as their income after taking the seminar and (for 15 students) participating in one-on-one mentoring phone calls with me once each month for three months. Of the four students who started with debt, all were debt-free within six months of attending the seminar.

This book tells their stories and explains how a few simple financial principles can be applied by young adults today to begin building a strong foundation for complete financial independence. My goal for you is that you won't have to depend on your parents for money by the time you finish reading this book and doing the exercises. If you are willing to work, you will find ways to make money for yourself, and you'll be financially stable and on the road to true financial independence before you even enter college. The main point is this: even as a "kid," you have more control over your financial situation then you (or your parents) realize. You need cash for cars, college, and clothes right now, and someday for a home, family, business, and (if you can bring yourself to imagine ever reaching your grandparents' age!) retirement. Get started now, and you can soar in the sun later, just like my hawk and me.

How Money Moves

Here you are, reading this crazy money book, with a whole $5.23 to your name and wondering how on earth you are ever going get any more money. I mean, your birthday isn't for another ten months! Thank heavens for Grandma, right? You always manage to score at least a few bucks in her annual birthday card! But what about now? You are broke, and you don't see any immediate hope in sight for a major change in your financial situation – except maybe down!

Take heart, my friend. All is not lost. Here are the details you need to get cash started rolling your way today.

The Nature of Money

First, let's talk about the real nature of money. How you use money will depend entirely on your perceptions of it. You have preconceived biases that you have absorbed from the world around you.

The big question here is simple. Do you see money as good or evil? Do you want to have more cash because you can use it to buy things that you or people in your life need or want? Or are you afraid of having too much money because the only people who seem to have lots of it are the folks who have done something bad to get it? These are some of the first questions you need to ask yourself. If you see money as a necessary "evil," your ability to find and save money, let alone use it wisely, will be colored by your negative view of what it can do. Money is not evil. Money is only a tool, like a hammer. You can use that hammer the right way, to build a house for someone who needs one. Or you can use it the wrong way, to smack someone up side the head. Either way, the hammer has no choice in how it is used. Good or bad, right or wrong, the choice – along with credit or blame – belongs solely to the one who wields it.

The same is true for money. Money is a useful tool, a medium of exchange that allows you to go to the mall and buy stuff you want. Money spends, regardless of how you get it. The bucks from Granny buy just as much as the cash you get for shoveling the driveway, or the coins you heisted from you twerp sister's piggy bank. The sales clerk and the shop owner don't care where you got the money; it spends. The only "good" or "bad" in money is what you bring to it.

If you think that money is "evil," take a minute to ask yourself some questions. "Why do I believe that money is evil?" "Is my view colored by how my parents handle cash?" "Do my friends have money, and do they use it well?" Write your answers down on a piece of paper, and then read them aloud to yourself. Why? Because as long as you believe that money is "bad" you will not be able to make or keep much of it

One student told me that the only wealthy people she had ever seen were in television programs or movies. She shared with me several examples that had led her to decide that the only way to get wealthy was to ignore others' needs and to abuse people's honesty. I responded that her warped view of fiscal reality was actually keeping her from making money. She was barely able to get by, living paycheck to paycheck while working and attending college. She had swallowed the myth shown in the media that bad people do wrong things to get rich at the expense of their good and hard-working but not-too-savvy neighbors. Without even thinking about it, she had adopted this view of "how money works in the real world" from shows produced in a realm of make-believe. Do you suffer from the same delusion? In order for each of us to be able to do what we need to do in life, we have to center our thoughts about money in the real world, and not in fantasy.

In every-day life in the real world, the rich people are the folks who keep communities together. They use their wealth in constructive and not destructive ways. They donate cash to good causes, they build businesses and employ others, they share their hard-won financial knowledge. They use the tool "money" in right ways to do good works. You can do so, too – if you want to.

So write down your assumptions about the nature of money. Is it good, or is it evil? If you ever have a lot of money, will you use it for the right reasons? What are some of the things you would do if you were wealthy? The point of this exercise is to allow you to make a decision. You have to give yourself permission to become wealthy. It doesn't make a difference what your parents or your friends think in this regard. You get to decide for yourself. If you have negative feelings about the making and using of money, you will sabotage your own attempts to gain it. If you see money as a tool to be used for good purposes as you see fit, then your efforts to find and keep cash will be rewarded with all the stuff you need now, and with ever increasing financial well-being in the future.

Are You Ready to Grow Up?

After you have read this book and completed the exercises, my goal for you is that you will be far along the road to financial maturity. You will have achieved a degree of understanding about money that many adults have yet to attain. In other words, you will have started to grow up.

Many of my young adult (and adult!) students have the wrong idea about what it means to become financially mature. When I ask young adults in my seminars to define how to know whether or not a person has reached financial maturity, their top three answers are:

1. When you get your first paying job,
2. When you have graduated from college, or
3. When you get married.

Being financially mature has nothing to do with these life events. Instead, it has everything to do with your mindset regarding the making, keeping, and spending of money. Your money.

A financially mature person (this means you!) will habitually exhibit five key behaviors. Together these traits will make you content now, and capable of real financial independence for the rest of your life. The five habits that all financially mature individuals possess are:

1. **You save.** You save because you understand the power of compound interest. A small amount of money set aside now and allowed to grow will produce a large bonus down the road.

2. **You mind your money matters.** You make your own money rather than using the "First Local Bank of Mom and Dad" as your preferred banking institution. Mom and Dad are not your personal ATM.

3. **You do your own work.** You are your own best financial advisor. Sure, you take advice from others, but deep down you know that you have to do your own research about how best to handle your hard-earned cash. Don't take the word of someone else. Study it for yourself.

4. **You keep going.** Every day you need to make decisions about your money, and some of them will be flat out wrong. Need to hear that again? You *will* make mistakes with your money; to not do so is impossible! But you will make the effort to correct them, and to not repeat them. Making mistakes is how we learn. By trying a short cut to riches and getting burned, you learn not to make that same error again! Don't avoid making a decision just because you're afraid of making a bad one. All financial decisions come with some degree of risk. The key is to watch what happens

after you make a decision, and learn. Resilience in the face of mistakes is maturity.

5. **Keep it simple.** You understand way down deep the old adage that "less is more." By knowing exactly what you want out of life, you will choose to spend your cash only on those needs and wants that bring you true pleasure. In this case, such simple pleasures mean more happiness – and all obtained for a lot less money!

By the end of this book you will know how to efficiently handle your money as it comes to you. And that, my young friend, is being mature!

Circles versus Lines

Most people see money in terms of a straight line. Remember geometry, where a starting point and an ending point can be used to define a line? To some people, money enters their life (the starting point), and then they spend it (the ending point); it passes through their hands (the line) and is gone before they even know what happened to it. You know the saying: "Easy come, easy go." This proverb when applied to money is absolutely wrong for two big reasons. First, the phrase "easy come" fools us into thinking that money can be had with little effort. No way! If you have a job, you know how hard you have to work to earn your cash (or what cash the tax man leaves you!); if you don't work, ask your parents how hard they have to work to feed, clothe, and shelter the family. Making money is not an "easy come" proposition. The ending phrase "easy go" is truer. Most of us see things we want, and we buy them without thinking. That said, the implication of the saying, that we have no control over how money moves through our lives, is not true. Almost all your choices about whether or not to keep or spend your cash are your own to make. We really do have control. It's just that most of us don't take the time to see it, let alone act on it.

Well, I'll let you in on a little known secret about money. The movement of money in our lives is actually circular, not linear. Money is always moving, and it comes and goes in cycles. This fact is reflected in another old adage: "It is better to give than to receive." Why? Because by giving stuff away you create a hole that is ready to be filled with new things, in this case the stuff you really need. Once you know how to follow the orbit of money, new opportunities for getting it will quite literally be pounding on your door as never before. No kidding!

How does this money thing work? Simple. Money has three phases or arms that require your attention. If you choose to correctly divide your money along these three paths from now on, you will see it accumulate in your life.

Here is a simple picture showing the circular path of money and how it will flow in a properly balanced life:

The Flow of Money

Living

Giving

Saving

The uppermost arrow is the "living" arm. Money in this branch takes care of basic needs we have such as food, clothing, and shelter. Most of my young adult students do not have to worry with living expenses right now because their parents are handling this aspect of their financial lives. For now, I figure that you also enjoy this benevolent situation, too, so for the moment I am going to assume that you don't have to pay for your own food, clothing, or rent. (If you do pay your own way, please see Appendix 1.)

Continuing down and to the right, the second arm of money is the "saving" branch. In order for money to flow to you, you have to keep some of it in reserve. Many people have heard over and over again of this need to save, but *how* to do it correctly has eluded them. I'll be discussing the "how" with you in later chapters.

Going on around to the left, the third division of money deals with "giving." It is an accepted fact that what you give to others will come back to you in kind. People have an intuitive understanding of this. You hear it all the time in our proverbs, such as:

What goes around comes around.
What you sow, that shall you reap.
Like begets like.

In fact, you probably use these principles yourself every single day. For example, if you want people to be polite to you, you use your manners with them first.

The same basic principle holds true for money, but for some reason people don't seem to get it. If you want money to come into your life, you must first give some of it away.

What is important for you right now is that you come to recognize the real nature of money in your life. Simply put, money moves, and does so in a cycle. How can you control the flow of money? Ah, now that is the million dollar question, isn't it? All you have to do is divide the money you receive so that it keeps your cash circulating. And that is the subject of the next chapter.

Running in Circles

So if money moves in circles, how do we track and capture the wily beast? Easy. Go fishing. First you gather some equipment and bait. Then you bait the hook, drop it in the water, and haul in what takes a bite. In terms of money, the "equipment" is how you make money, the "bait" is the cash you set aside, and the "hooks" are the set of financial tools you will use to put your cash to work for you. The idea is the same, whether you are fishing for dinner or dinero.

The 40/60 Principle

Easy enough in concept, you say, but how does it really work? I'm glad you asked because it is a piece of cake. As a young adult, the single universal key to making your money work as hard for you as you do for it is to follow the 40/60 Principle.

Now, now, don't freak out. The 40/60 Principle is not some clever trick to make you learn math. In fact, you don't need much math at all to use this technique to your advantage. The idea behind the 40/60 Principle is that you divide your money among several main uses in a very defined and focused manner. When you have put the right amount of money into each of these categories, you engage universal laws of wealth accumulation that start the flow of money into your life. Lots of money.

Interested? Then let's see how it all works. For this principle to succeed in your life, you will need to split your money into five portions. A simple way to understand this system is to visualize it using a five-pointed star:

Each point of the star represents a potential use that you will make of your money.

The topmost star point reflects the part of your cash that you use in "living" every day. Everyone recognizes that the primary reason we want money is to buy stuff that we need or desire. Money is a medium of exchange that the community has adopted to make business transactions easier. Naturally, then, if you want to be involved in buying or selling, you will need to have access to some cash.

So far, so good. Of course you need to use some of your money to live. Unfortunately, a big problem with this "living" arm of the money cycle is that many people focus only on this one aspect of their financial well-being. They live paycheck to paycheck, spending all their money on stuff and forgeting to allot any of it to the other four star points.

Ignoring these other four areas is a certain invitation to fiscal disaster, since in doing so you break the universal laws which keep money flowing into your life. Spending all the money that comes to you as soon as you get it leaves you with no means of meeting those unforeseen expenses that crop up from time to time. Things like new tires for your ride, or a faster computer, or a college education. (Trust me, tuition bills always come due when you least expect them!) So if you just have to have whatever it is, you purchase it on credit. And therein lies your doom. Buying stuff using borrowed cash gives you not only the thing you wanted but a nice little debt to go with it. And for many people the debt outlasts the item – which means you end up paying even more in the long run. Sure, money doesn't buy happiness, but having it around really helps! And the best way of keeping it close is to remember to include the other four branches of the 40/60 Principle when dividing your money.

The two points on the lower right of the star stand for "savings," which is that part of your hard-won cash that you keep for yourself. You have heard the old adage, "It takes money to make money." Well, your "savings" is the seed money you need to make some of your hard work to get money start paying you back. The "savings" portion of the money cycle is divided into two branches: long-term and short-term. (Hence the two star points; tricky, huh?) You might ask, "What's the big difference? I mean, savings is savings, right?" Wrong. You use long-term and short-term savings for different things.

Your long-term savings is the money you are setting aside for far-distant expenses. Stuff like your retirement in 50 years, or college educations for your own kids. Sure, if you are 12 years old and reading this book, 50 years in the future seems like a long time. Well, it's not. The reason you want to start saving now is a little known financial miracle called compound interest. We'll consider this mathematical law in greater detail in a later chapter. For now, know that the principle of compound interest means that a small amount of cash put by now will grow to be tens or hundreds of times as much by the time you need it in the far distant future. And a big hoard of cash is how most of us decide whether or not we have become financially independent. The key to your long-term savings is that you want to save early, save often, and not touch it until decades from now. Do this regularly and you will accumulate a substantial degree of wealth in your lifetime. And you won't even feel deprived!

In contrast, your short-term savings is a "rainy day" fund created to pay for those little unexpected incidents that life just keeps throwing your way. Expenses that fall in this category include things that you have to pay once or a few times each and every year, like insurance premiums or tax bills for your car, and sudden emergencies, like a broken electric guitar or the need to score some tickets to a hot new concert. Some other examples of major expenses that you will want to pay from your short-term savings include buying a car or attending college. In all these cases, the primary issue is not how large the expense is, but how soon you have to pay it. That is why your car and your own college education fall to the short-term arm of savings.

Finally, the two star points to the lower left reflect the "giving" component of the money cycle. I can hear you now. "Say what? I went out and busted my backside to earn some cash, and now I'm supposed to give it away?" Yep, that's what I'm saying. Them that gives, gets. You already know that this principle is true. If you are polite to people, they usually are polite to you in return. If you give someone a gift, at some time they will give you one. The same tenet holds true for your money. If you give something of yourself, you have shown the Universe that you are not just in it for yourself. And, the Universe will remember.

So how does "giving" work? As with your "saving" plans, your "giving" efforts are divided into two portions. The first is philanthropy. A lot of people call this "charity," but the two practices are quite different. *Charity* is the free gift of any good or service to an organization or a person without any anticipation of reward. *Philanthropy* is the free gift of money without expecting a return. Charity is giving away stuff or time (which only indirectly can be counted as money), while philanthropy is the direct donation of your hard-earned cash. So who really cares? You do, because the Universe pays you back *in kind*. If you want to get food, give people cookies or buy them a meal. If you want to receive cold hard cash, give money. Simple but powerful. Don't make the mistake of being stingy in this area of your financial life.

So where do you send your philanthropic monies? You donate them to a worthy cause that is doing good works. The possibilities are infinite; you will be able to find hundreds of organizations in your community, your state, throughout the country and the entire world. You can find their names in newspapers, magazines, on the Internet. Just pick one that does a service that you think is important. The point is not where you give, but that you give.

The other aspect of your "giving" effort is to donate money to an organization that seeks to share your beliefs with the world. Most people carry out this requirement by giving their money to their church. The name by which the donation is called is irrelevant (examples include tithing, temple dues, faith offerings, or heart gifts); the point is that you share some of your money to perpetuate your values. What if you don't belong to an established church? Do you get to keep the money? Nope. You take the amount you would have donated for this purpose and direct it to a philanthropic organization.

The point of giving in this way is to show the Universe that some of the money coming into your life is going to be used to help the people around you. After all, your mom and dad have been telling you to share your toys for years. (I know that I heard this at least a million times before I left home as an 18-year-old!) Why should this basic principle be any different with money?

How to Cut the Cheese

Okay, so you need to divvy up your money into five portions. (It's okay to whimper about it, just a little, as long as you actually do it.) So how much goes where? The answer to that question is in the 40/60 Principle. And by the way, this is where the math kicks in. (C'mon, it's money. You knew that there had to be math in here somewhere!) But don't sweat it. The math is simple.

The first thing to do is to get some money by some honest enterprise. That cash, however much it is, represents a value of 100%. Now you split it into five parts, like this:

40% goes to Living. You care for yourself with this money.

Obviously the 40% is the "40" part of the 40/60 Principle. The remaining 60%, then, is clearly tied to the "60" part. It gets carved up in this fashion:

40% goes to Savings. You use this money to prepare for your future. Now you divide this portion into two chunks, like this:

> *20% goes to Short-term Savings.* This cash is set aside to pay for large expenses that are not expected or occur only on occasion. You need this to avoid going deep into debt.

> *20% goes to Long-term Savings.* You will use these funds to care for yourself and your family once you are no longer interested in or able to work. This foresight will prevent you from becoming a liability to those who share your world (your kids, community, or country). Do this early and often, and leave the money alone to grow, and you will find yourself on Easy Street later in life.

20% goes to Giving. This money is shared with those around you to make the world a better place for all. This part gets split into two pieces, like this:

10% goes to a Philanthropy of your choice. This cash demonstrates your willingness to share the good things that the Universe has given you – thereby showing that you can be trusted to continue receiving (and sharing) in the good things of the world.

10% goes to a Spiritual Institution of your choice. This money is like the "rent" you pay to the Universe for giving you a healthy body that eats, breathes, and enjoys the fun to be had here on the planet Earth! You may complain about the size and shape and color of the body you were given, but, hey, you did get one, and there is a charge! If you do not have a formal affiliation with a church, then take this 10% and give it to philanthropy. The point is to keep the money cycle flowing.

The end result of all this money allocation is this:

Living (40%)

Tithing (10%)

Short-term Savings (20%)

Philanthropy (10%)

Long-term Savings (20%)

The math is easy, and the rule is simple. The 40/60 Principle is powerful. Use it as a young adult, and continue doing so as an adult, and you will never want for cash. Better yet, you will have a great start toward a goal that most people only dream of: financial independence.

The Piggy Bank Principle

So now you know. You can really rock your world in the financial sense if you just keep the 40/60 Principle in mind. But while it's is all well and good to talk about how money moves and what you're supposed to do with it, how do you really get the process going? What is that one easy thing you can do to kick-start the whole cycle of money in your life? Well, here it is.

I call this exercise the Piggy Bank Principle. I do so because you gather up all the money you own that is not in some bank account, starting with your piggy bank. Go to all the places that you stash stuff and dig out every dollar, dime, and penny that you possess (but leave your siblings' banks alone!). Now, add it all up. Most of the young adults who I have mentored tell me that this money quest provides them with $3 to $15. Okay, now you are going to prime the pump of your personal money cycle by dividing your cash among the different categories we just discussed.

As an example, let's say you scrounged around and managed to find $5.25 in your secret hoards of cash. Now we start by figuring out how much money is yours to spend (the "Living" arm of your personal money cycle), using the following simple calculation:

$$\$5.25 \times 0.4 = \$2.10$$

The term "0.4" is the mathematical way of writing "40%" in an equation. So make change from your money pile, and put $2.10 in your wallet to buy stuff you need or want.

Next you figure out how much money needs to go into your two savings accounts. Yes, you really will have to have *two* savings accounts. One holds your cash for long-term needs, while the other houses your money for larger, short-term projects and emergencies. Again, the calculation is easy:

$$\$5.25 \times 0.2 = \$1.05$$

Again, the "0.2" term means "20%" in this equation. Now, put $1.05 into *each* of your savings accounts. "Wait just a minute," you might fire back. "What if I don't have any

30

savings accounts?" Good question. Put your cash into two envelopes labeled "Long-term" and "Short-term" and hold your savings in them until you have accumulated enough money to open your accounts at your local bank.

Finally, let's figure out the amounts you need to direct into your religious and philanthropic organizations:

$$\$5.25 \text{ X } 0.1 \text{ } = 52.5 \text{ ¢}$$

(Okay, all together now. What does the "0.1" term mean? That's right, "10%.") Well, since we don't cut pennies in half these days, the next best thing to do is to round and give 53¢ to your church and 52¢ to philanthropy (or else 52¢ to your church and 53¢ to philanthropy). Either division is fine as long as you share. Again, place your gifts into envelopes labeled "Spiritual" and "Philanthropic" until you actually have the opportunity to deliver them.

One note regarding your savings accounts, the amount of cash you need to open a savings account at your local bank is usually $5 to $25 if you're under 18 years of age. Banks keep these initial deposits low on purpose to attract your business. Once you are at the bank, check with them to find out how much money you need to open a checking account as well. Why? Because you need to learn how to use checks and checkbooks. (Debit cards, too, which look like credit cards but work like checks. Money is pulled straight from your checking account when you use it.) It is always easier to develop a good habit if you start it while young – especially if it has to do with money. Start the saving accounts first, and when you have enough money to do so you can open your checking account. The experience of using checks (or debit cards) to pay expenses and of balancing your own checkbook against the bank statement each month is a great way to begin learning habits of financial maturity and independence. Better still, you can do so in a setting in which help (Mom or Dad) is available to assist you in understanding the ins and outs of the world of money.

Why Pump Priming Works

As I told you above, the essence of the Piggy Bank Principle is priming the pump of your own money cycle. How does this work? Simple. What you have done by dividing your spare cash among the different portions of the 40/60 Principle is show the Universe that you are going to be responsible in the use of your cash, both for yourself and for the sake of others. You have said, "From now on,

I'm going to use some of my money in living today, save some of it to help me live well tomorrow, and give some of it to others to help make the world around me a better place." Such actions serve the same purpose as ringing a bell to get the attention of a desk clerk. Hit the bell, and the clerk comes to give you help. Prime your financial pump and you will notice that money starts coming into your life. When you get these new "batches" of money, do the exact same thing all over again: divide the cash according to the 40/60 Principle, and wait for the next influx of money. My young adult (and adult!) students have told me that within a week of breaking into their piggy banks people started giving them cash, or hiring them for odd jobs, or asking to buy something they had been trying to sell unsuccessfully for months. I can't predict in what way the Universe will bring money into your life, but I do know that money will flow to you.

One thing to remember. Just as soon as new money enters your life, split it up using the 40/60 Principle. Don't wait for later, because chances are that you will forget if you delay. If you break the flow of money by keeping it all for yourself, even if by accident, then the broken cycle will stop bringing money your way. Don't let money sit around. It likes to flow!

Exercise 1: Get all your cash that is not held in a bank account. Divide it according to the 40/60 Principle. Go on! Do it now! (Yes, you can use a calculator!)

Exercise 2: As soon as more money comes to you, repeat Exercise 1. Now, you're on your way!

"I Found my Porpoise!"

So, you have some money burning a hole in your pocket. It's the 40% of your money that you can use for your day-to-day needs and wants. Just because you have money doesn't mean you really know what to do with it. So how do you play the money game to win?

The first thing to do is to stop and ask yourself a question: "What do I really want from life?" Write down your answers. (Are you writing?) You want to do this because if you don't know what you want from life, how will you know whether or not the item you want to buy is something you really need? Remember, you work hard for your money, so you want to make every cent count. I want you to have as much happiness as you can get throughout life, and the wise use of money is a major factor in how happy we feel. Yet at the same time I want you to be able to save enough money to meet your future expenses, while avoiding the feeling that you have to exist in a lifelong state of deprivation. So, how do you balance all these things?

This principle is so simple that most people miss it. *Know exactly what you want out of life.* That's it. Figure out where you are going and what you need to get there, and then only spend your money on things that will help you move along the way.

Let's take an example. Say you have $10 in your pocket. One day you find yourself at the mall with some friends, and they decide that they want something to eat. You go along because you enjoy their company, even though you're not very hungry yourself. What's the best thing for you to do with your money? Buy lunch anyway and then leave most of it on the plate, or have a glass of water while you chat with your friends as they eat? What is the primary point of being with your friends? Is it to spend time talking, laughing, and enjoying their company, or is it to spend your hard-earned money? In most cases we are actually seeking the companionship and not the cooking. So be conscious about what your real needs are in life, and you will keep more of your money. By asking yourself the quick question "What do I actually want?" when faced with a possible purchase, you quickly lead yourself down a path of reasoning that shows you how to best spend – or keep – your cash.

Focusing Your Financial Future

Now some of you might be saying, "Hold on a sec. That $10 is from my "living" allowance, the 40% of my cash that I can spend on myself in any way that I choose. Why can't I go out to eat with my friends?" Well, no one will stop you, unless you do. Sure, you are able to spend that $10, but don't you want it to go as far as it can, and only be spent on things that add real meaning to your life? If the answer to this question is "Yes," then you need to get in the habit of asking yourself, "What do I really want?"

What I'm trying to do with you right now is to help you figure out what is your primary purpose in life. Why? Simple. To keep more of your "living" money in your own pocket until you spend it on something really good.

Students of all ages have told me that by knowing their real purpose in life they have been able to decrease the amount of money they spend on a whim. This tendency toward unplanned purchases is called impulse buying, and it is a huge source of revenue for companies in the United

States. Firms spend millions of dollars on research each year to learn the best way to separate you from your money. The most effective means of countering their ingenious advertising campaigns is to know up front whether or not a potential impulse buy actually will serve your purpose.

So what is a purpose suitable for a lifetime? In particular, your lifetime. To me, a good purpose is a task that you want to do that will make life better, either for yourself, your family, or folks in the community (and ideally for all three). We're not talking about what sort of job or career you want to have. We are not discussing the activity that you do to *make* your money. We're talking about the thing that you want to do because you enjoy it more than anything else in the world, a task that brings you pleasure and helps other people, too! Do you want to start a band? Buy toys for sick kids at the local hospital? Educate people your own age on how to build their own website? Build the next dot.com megabusiness? Whatever you like to do with your time that serves more people than just yourself is your life's purpose.

Most people glide through life with no conscious idea that there is (or at least should be) more to living then eating, sleeping and working. Amazing, isn't it? In horror movies such individuals are called "zombies." Don't be one of them. Break out of this mold and decide to do something with your life that gives you a sense of purpose and at the same time is something that you really have fun doing. You have probably heard the saying that goes "If you love what you do on the job, you'll never work a day in your life." This adage is a true law of the Universe. Find your purpose and you'll never "work" again, no matter how hard the tasks you perform in the course of a day. Better yet, the true reward for your effort comes in the pleasure of the job itself. The money is an added benefit. This is the kind of life you want to make for yourself, because such contentment is worth more than all the money in the world.

Do What You Like, the Money Will Come

One of my young adult students really enjoys listening to family stories. She began by recording tales that her grandmother and grandfather told her about their own childhood in rural Mississippi. One year as a Christmas gift she handed out these stories in a book to all of her family members. She now goes around to different people in her community and in retirement homes listening to the stories these folks have to tell about their lives. In fact, she is now working on her third book, one that focuses on women who worked during World War II in the factories of Detroit. She has found her purpose. She is an author. She calls herself a verbal historian. She really enjoys interviewing people to help catalogue their knowledge for future generations. This "job" gives her a fulfilling life that leaves her happy because she knows she is contributing to the history of her country. By the way, her books are in high demand, so her chosen "career" also makes her loads of money!

Now, your thing may not be writing at all. Maybe you want to become the best electric guitar player who ever lived. Or maybe a marine biologist, or a public servant, or a stay-at-home parent. Fine. The point is this: think about what you want to do with your time, and how your chosen activity will keep money flowing into your life. You want it to be something that you enjoy, but that also serves other people. Playing music helps others to forget their own troubles while allowing you to be creative. Starting that band allows many people to get together to play music, form friendships, and make some money, too! (Although your parents may argue with you over whether or not what you are playing in the basement should be classified as "Music!") Even a stay-at-home parent whose main joy in life is caring for the family can harness the power of the money cycle, either by doing some form of paying work at home (like free-lance writing, medical transcription, or serving as the community Tupperware salesperson) or by learning how to cut expenses to the bone. The point is that the old proverb is true: do what you love, and the money will follow.

Moreover, by knowing your purpose in life you will stop spending money wastefully on things that do not add to your real happiness. By having a goal that is bigger than yourself, you come to know that the reason you have cash is not to hoard it or to spend it selfishly on material things, but rather to do something that will make this world a better place and allow you to have fun at the same time. Is that cool, or what? Finding your purpose and following it is the best way I know to prevent you from impulse buying. You'll stop and think, "Hey, do I really want that new computer game, or do I want to save my money for that new amplifier the band needs?" Your choices will be better. Your "living" money will go farther. You will be reaching your goals. You will be truly content. And that, my friend, is the name of the game.

In Your Sight, In Your Mind

Another old saying with a lot of truth to it is the one that goes, "Out of sight, out of mind." The reason I bring this up is that you need to find a way to constantly remind yourself of your purpose in life, or you will forget it. But how do you do this? Create a visual reminder of your purpose, one that will spring readily to your mind's eye even if you are far away for long periods of time. Here is how to go about it.

During one financial seminar I held for youth I was explaining the power of purpose and told the students that the best way to stay true to their goals was to have a three-dimensional object they could look at from time to time. This object could be anything as long as it reminded them of their purpose and would provide them with immediate visual remembrance of their reason for working hard in life.

After the lunch break I found a plain brown paper bag on the podium. I was a bit hesitant to open it since many of the kids in the room were trying hard to stifle giggles. I also had the fleeting impression that there might be something alive and slimy in the bag. I need not have worried. When I finally plunged my hand into the sack, I pulled it back to find this small stuffed Dolphin. My mind was totally filled with questions marks at this point. Finally, a sweet young voice called from the back of the room, "Mrs. Bolon, I just wanted to let you know that I found my porpoise!" All the kids laughed, and I joined them. All of us realized that a porpoise was a great three-dimensional object for helping to keep one's own noble purpose clearly in mind. I was also tickled that everyone in the classroom had understood the importance of finding their own great purpose.

A year later another student approached me with his three-dimensional object. It had taken him a few months of hard thinking to pull together his purpose, and he wanted to show me what he had worked up. As he told me his plans for music and pulling together a band with a unique sound, he unveiled the picture he was carrying. It was a framed gold CD on a black velvet background. I was so proud that he had never given up on his dream. No matter that forming a band is hard. He had recognized that this was his dream, and also his purpose in life, and so he had chosen an object to give him a real target to shoot for … a solid gold album!

It doesn't matter what three-dimensional object you choose to keep your purpose in mind, as long as it matters to you. Pick a good vivid object like a porpoise or a gold CD, and then each time you're out and about you will be able to stop yourself when presented with a sudden impulse to spend money and automatically ask whether or not the proposed purchase is really worth delaying your purpose. This simple technique works to keep more of your money in your pocket to use on the things that will really give you pleasure by advancing your purpose. The whole idea can be summed up using the words spoken by a doomed Rebel commander during the climactic assault on the Death Star during the original *Star Wars* movie: "Stay on target."

Don't be discouraged if you don't know "what you want to be when you grow up." Pick a good purpose, and stick with it – even if it just for now. Your purpose as a young adult may start off really mundane, like saving cash for a car or a computer or to start your own web-based business. But as more money comes into your life and as you grow and begin to seek farther afield for opportunities to make money, you'll see things in your community or your country or even the world that you want to impact. And then before you know it...you have a porpoise!

Exercise 3: Write down the answers to these questions.

What is it that I would do with my time if I could choose to do whatever I wanted?

What types of activities would really make me excited to get out of bed each morning?

What are ten things that I could do to make money?

Now, pick three money-making opportunities from that list of ten that you would really *enjoy*. This list is the foundation of your purpose. Start here to decide what you are going to do now to serve your community and make money, too!

Using It Today: The Living Branch of the Money Cycle

Now that you know how to split your money using the 40/60 Principle and you have some idea about what your purpose in life will be (at least for now), let's spend a few moments considering the best ways to really use your "living" money. Using money is not "see it, want it, get it." You know that you will have plenty of choices to make when deciding when, where, and how to spend your money. Carefully considering those options to make good decisions allows you to stretch your dollars even further, and will provide the very best means of maximizing the pleasure and performance of the things that you need to buy. Other than making the best use of your cash, why should you care? Well, try these statistics on for size.

In 2004, teenagers (youths between the ages of 13 to 18 years) had approximately $5,200 to spend, gotten either by their own job-related efforts or from the generosity of their parents. That figure represents the national average for the entire United States. In case you were wondering, $5200 is a lot of money to spend (at any age)! And dollars will get you donuts that much of that money was wasted, because many purchases probably contributed little or nothing to the happiness or usefulness of the teens who spent it. So what do you do? How do you keep from wasting your hard-earned cash? You develop the habit of frugality.

The Right State of Mind

Now, frugality is a grand old word that has fallen out of fashion. Most folks today, upon hearing the words "frugal" or "frugality," use words such as "cheapskate" or "tightwad" or "miser" as a substitute. But frugality is not a simple matter of being cheap. Instead, *frugality* is a mindset that you will pay good money for good value, but only if that value serves a noble purpose: increasing the happiness of you or your family, or improving the lot of your friends and neighbors. Misers don't spend money. Frugal people spend money on things of value, but only after very careful consideration of what they are buying. As you grow older, you will come to recognize that you will best be able to use the 40% of your money by developing a deliberately frugal mindset.

The most straightforward method of acquiring and keeping this frugal mindset is to track all of your expenses and all of your income. Start doing it now. In doing so you will automatically develop the habit of frugality, and you will be able to use it to make sure that you only buy things that you truly need. Don't groan, my friend, it isn't as hard as you think!

The issue with money is that most people have no idea how much money they have to work with. By tracking the way money flows through your life you will soon get a crystal-clear picture of the amounts of money you have to play with on a weekly and monthly basis. One of my 12-year-old students was shocked to find out that over the course of three months he had access to over $300. Sure, some of the money was given to him by his parents to buy books and school supplies, but a lot of it was his to use as he saw fit. Because he had never tracked money before, he had no idea how much money passed through his hands. The simple act of writing down and regularly reviewing the amount of money he could spend made him conscious of the many options he had for purchasing things to fill his life – and helped him judge which ones he really needed.

Tracking the Wily Beast

The first thing most of my students complain of (even my adult ones!) when I tell them to track all their expenses is that it sounds like it will be either boring or hard, or both. I have two comebacks to these thoughts. The first is that I am willing to be bored if, by doing so, I can save myself hundreds or thousands of dollars in bad buys. So far, no one has been able to argue that point with me. After all, the whole reason for the money game is to make sure that you get the most for your cash and still supply your needs.

As for the second point, tracking your money is not hard. You only have to record what you bought, and how much you paid for it. Over time you can use these records to figure out what represents a good price for those items you buy on a regular basis, like sodas or guitar picks. That way you learn to always buy them at the lowest possible price.

If my 12-year-old student from the above example can do it, so can you. Tracking your expenses is quite easy. Make or buy a notebook (any size will do, though a small spiral-bound one that you can take with you to the store is a good choice). Every time you get or spend money, write it in your notebook. Once you get used to recording all your expenses in this way you'll be surprised at how automatic and easy it becomes. Below is a sample sheet from one of my students:

Mary's Expenses:

Date	Description	Total Received	40% for Living	Total for Living
10/15	Money in Piggy Bank	$8.01	$3.20	$3.20
10/18	Birthday money	$10.00	$4.00	$7.20
11/1	Candy for friend and me		-$2.18	$5.02
11/15	Money for clothes from Mom and Dad	$250.00	$250.00	$255.02
12/10	Babysitting money	$20.00	$8.00	$263.02
12/19	Christmas gifts		-$12.68	$250.34

See, there are no fancy tricks or maths needed to track your expenses and your income. You want to know where your money is going and where it is coming from. Keeping a list is the only way you will be able to get a handle on it.

Now, did you see the one discrepancy in the sample list above? Mary got one big wad of money, $250, from her parents to buy clothes, and she did not split it according to the 40/60 Principle. If she had, her entry would have reflected $100 (40% of $250) rather than the full amount. Instead she put all $250 into her "living" fund because she was responsible for purchasing her own clothes for the winter. The reason she did not apply the 40/60 split to this money was that she did not earn it for herself or get it as a gift. It was her parents' cash and not her own. More importantly, her "failure" to allocate it by the 40/60 Principle did not break the flow of money. If someone gives you money for a very specific purpose, you do not have to apply the 40/60 Principle to it. For example, a relative may give you some money and tell you that it is for your college fund. If this happens, then put it in your short-term savings account and keep it there for college. You honor the requests of the people giving you the money

However, the table also shows that each time new money of her own came into Mary's life from her "job" (babysitting) or from any other source (such as her birthday money), she would act without fail to allocate 40% to her "living" needs and divide the remaining 60% among her various accounts. You will need to do this, too, to keep money flowing in your life. The tracking log for recording income and expenses is a great way of getting a handle on the 40% of your money that you can use for "living."

Keep in mind the point of this tracking exercise. Do you remember what it is? By tracking all your expenses you will save yourself money. How? Because the act of tracking forces you to slow down your thought processes with respect to money; it makes you really think about whether or not you need or just want that gizmo that is calling to you as you walk through the mall. In short, the tracking prevents you from impulse buying, because you actually get embarrassed for yourself when you waste your money on things that don't help you to move closer to achieving your purpose in life.

The easiest way to save your money is not to spend it in the first place. Keep that in mind before you decide to moan that tracking is boring or hard. Just do it, and sit back and watch your expenses fall while your stash for "living" mounts up until you really need it.

Give Credit Its Due

As young adults you will soon be exposed to the joys and hardships of credit cards and other forms of debt. Credit cards have their place. They are a good way to get a small loan – but only if you know absolutely that you can pay it all back when your statement arrives. By using a credit card you can purchase an item today and not pay for it until the month ends. At times this freedom is convenient, like if you need to score concert tickets for this weekend but you don't get your paycheck for another two weeks. That said, *under no circumstances* should you use a credit card to buy something if you won't have the money available to pay it back at once. The last thing you want to have as a young adult (or even as an "old" person like me) is a growing pile of credit card debt and the ever-mounting monthly interest charges that go along with it. Such debts can take months or years to pay off, especially if you can't pay more than the bare minimum payment each month.

So what, you say? Well, most young adults with credit card debt earn just enough money to make that low minimum payment. That means that they aren't working to live, but just working to pay off things that already entered – and likely already left – their life. Keep a credit card for sudden emergencies if you must, but don't just whip it out without thinking hard about what you really want in life. You want to fulfill a great purpose and become financially independent (or else you wouldn't be reading this book!). Just say "No way" to casual credit card use, and properly divide your money. Use cash when you can, and keep the plastic in the purse.

Exercise 4: Purchase or make a portable notebook in which to record your expenses and income. Track every transaction! Review your list at least once each month to find patterns in your financial life that can help you to keep more of your money (like buying your sodas in the cheaper 2-liter bottles rather than in more expensive 12-ounce cans, or only buying bottles of soda when the price falls below a given level).

Holding It for Tomorrow: The
Saving Branch of the Money Cycle

Okay, so now you have your purpose, and you have started splitting your new incoming money using the 40/60 Principle, and you will be tracking your money flow from now on. So far, so good. That takes care of living today. But what about living tomorrow? You don't want to be cruising along and suddenly find that your accumulated assets aren't adequate when tomorrow finally arrives. Since 40% of your income is going to get dumped into savings, let's take a few pages to really pound in the fine art of saving today to build an excellent tomorrow.

Remember from above that you will actually need two separate savings accounts, one for long-term needs and one for short-term emergencies. The two accounts serve different functions, both of which must be attended to if your financial ship is to be truly worthy of weathering the financial storms in the ocean of life.

Baby Steps to Meet Big Needs

All right, so you aren't a baby any more. I'm sorry for dredging up that entire childhood trauma. But the concept of baby steps is a powerful way of visualizing the purpose of your short-term savings account.

The relevance of baby steps to a young adult like you is that you will only to be able to add a few dollars (or dimes) to your account when you are first starting to go out and get money. It may seem like no big deal, but a few bucks of birthday or babysitting money added to the stash now and then can build a fairly good chunk of change by the time you need it a few years later. This capacity to hold your money until you need it is the whole reason for having a short-term savings account: a place to park cash until you suddenly need lots of it in the future to buy some big-ticket item. Like a car, or tuition, or prom clothes, or even exotic travel (which are the usual hot items that my young adult students mention in my classes). You also use this account for the emergencies that come up every now and then.

One 14-year-old student told me how he needed his mountain bike repaired after a small fender bender with a fence. (I didn't ask him how he managed to run into a six-foot-high, chain-link fence which presumably couldn't get around on its own. I'm your fiscal mentor and not your mom, right?) Anyhow, he hadn't expected that *little* incident, and it wound up costing him $85 to get his bike back on line. This unexpected expense had to be paid immediately because he had his own business and used his bike to deliver the products to his customers. It was a good thing for him that he had been splitting his income using the 40/60 Principle for the last few months, since he had $98 sitting in his short-term savings account to cover the sudden repair costs.

Your short-term savings account is also there to keep you from getting into trouble if you need to use credit cards to cover big expenses. Having a stash of ready cash in the bank allows you to use the card with confidence since you already know that you can pay the debt in full at the end of the month. That said, a good habit to live by at any age, but especially for young adults like you, is "pay to play." If you don't have the cash in hand (or in bank) to pay for it now, just put the item back and walk away.

Choose Who Will Do the Work for You

Your other means to build cash for later use is a long-term savings account. You probably have heard this account referred to as a "pay yourself first" account, or a "nest egg" account. Money in such accounts is there to help you with your "living" expenses when you can no longer work. Believe it or not, a day will come in your life about 50 years from now when you want to (or have to) retire. So why should you care? This may be the first time in your life that someone has mentioned the concept of retirement to you, so it can't be very important for you right now, can it? Ah, my young apprentice, read and learn. The purpose behind starting a long-term savings account now and contributing to it on a regular basis has to do with the *power of compound interest*. What that all boils down to is: *you can have your money work hard for you starting now, or you can work hard later to get more money.* Your call, of course, but if I were you (and I was at one time, so I speak from experience as a former young adult!) I would give some thought to taking the easy road just this once.

Einstein (remember him, the most famous scientist of the last century?) was most impressed with the concept of money earning money. He even aided our understanding of how money grows by creating the "Rule of 72." (Okay, since I mentioned it, I guess I should tell you; the Rule says that 72 divided by the interest rate your money is earning will tell you how long it will be in years before the money you have in the bank will double. Now, back to work!) Even though his profession had nothing to do with money, Einstein saw the power of compound interest. In fact, he thought that it was "the greatest mathematical discovery of all time." Fortunately for those of us who want to be financially independent, he was right! Better yet, we don't all have to be geniuses like him to use it!

So, if you're going to take advantage of this math miracle, you should probably know something about what it means. And guess what? Once you do, you will never be tempted to skip the 40/60 Principle when you get new cash, and you will never ever allow yourself to become buried in credit card debt. Simply stated, compound interest is the process by which your money *and the money you earn by investing it* grow over time. Whenever you invest or borrow money, the original cash (called the "principal") is used for a defined length of time (called the "term") in exchange for a small fee (called "interest"). The fee is a set percentage (called the "interest rate") of the principal amount. The key to getting rich is to add the interest payment to the principal amount, because a higher principal earns more money. This secret is why credit card companies earn such high fees.

Let's take a simple example. Say you put $10.00 into your savings account for one year, and the bank pays interest of 10% compounded annually. The first year you would earn:

$$\$10.00 \times 0.1 = \$1.00$$

(Remember that the "0.1" term is the mathematical way of saying "10%" in an equation.) You're probably thinking, "Big deal. One lousy buck." But wait. If you leave your money in the bank, the power of compound interest kicks in, because next year your principal is $11 (your original $10 plus $1 in interest you earned):

$$\$11.00 \times 0.1 \ (10\%) = \$1.10$$

And so on. One important thing to remember when playing with compound interest is that the rate determines the speed at which your money grows. For example …

Graph 1: Growth of $100 Invested for 20 Years

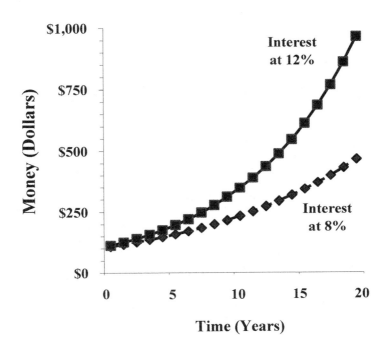

This figure is based on a one-time contribution of $100 put into and held in an account that pays a constant (or "fixed") rate of interest (either 8% or 12%) for 20 years. You can plainly see that regardless of the specific interest rate both lines move upward in a curve, and not just as a line. Furthermore, you can tell that the largest amount of growth will occur in the *last five years*. That curve is the power of compounding. If you wait patiently, your money will start to grow exponentially, but you have to give it time to grow. Just like a tree. If you plant a seed and dig it up every day to see how it is doing, you will stunt its growth. Long-term savings works the same way. You have to plant your cash and leave it (i.e., *don't take it out and spend it!*) if you want your investment to keep on earning more money for you.

Now, I used the 8% and 12% interest rates to really prove this point about compound interest in a visually startling way. Keep in mind that the usual interest rate that banks pay in a normal economy is lots lower (from 1.5% to 6%), so the growth of your money over time will be slower. But it will grow! If you want to see your wealth grow more quickly, consider moving your cash from a regular savings account with a low rate of interest to an account (such as a stock or bond mutual fund) that pays a higher rate. Just remember that higher rates of return also carry higher rates of risk. Your nest egg might grow faster in a stock fund – but it also has a chance of shrinking. I'm not knocking stocks; I own them because they offer a better return. You just have to do your homework up front to know what your risks are before pursuing a higher payout on your principal.

Now, most people are not patient. Many folks get discouraged because the front portion of the compound interest curve looks pretty flat; they often think that nothing is happening. I want you to remember that patience is hard, but it will be rewarded. If the figure in Graph 1 is not enough proof for you, take a look at the figures in Table 1 (which shows the numbers used to make Graph 1).

Table 1: Growth of $100 Invested for 20 Years

Year	8% Interest	12% Interest
1	108	112
2	117	125
3	126	140
4	136	157
5	147	176
6	159	197
7	171	221
8	185	248
9	200	277
10	216	311
11	233	348
12	252	390
13	272	436
14	294	489
15	317	547
16	343	613
17	370	687
18	400	769
19	432	861
20	466	965

Once again see that the fastest growth in your cash occurs in the last five years. This pattern explains why your youth offers a tremendous advantage in your efforts to make your hard-earned money work for you! By starting to save now, you are giving your stash a chance to compound its growth for years. This extended term is critical, because the longer your money grows, the more you have at the end. Don't believe me? Well, this graph shows what occurs when that same $100 grows for 50 years instead of just 20.

Graph 2: $100 Invested for 50 Years

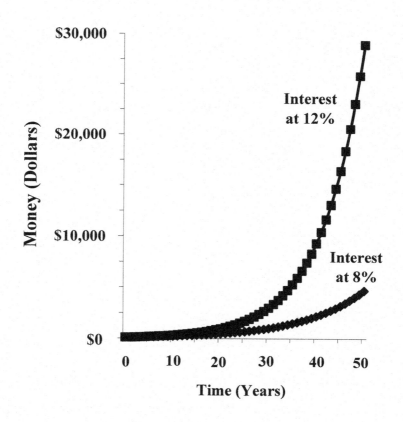

This figure shows that the upswing you saw in the curves in Graph 1 becomes ever more marked over time, especially for higher rates of interest. When you compare Graph 1 with Graph 2, the importance of time is immediately seen. When compounded annually at a rate of 12%, your initial $100 grew to about $1000 in 20 years but reached almost $30,000 after 50 years. That is why your youth is a major asset in your quest for financial independence – as long as you start saving now.

By the way, when you invest today, your typical rate of return will range between 4% to 5% (if held in bank accounts or used to buy bonds) to 9% or 10% (if used to purchase stocks or stock funds). So the main ingredient for success is to save early and save often. Get to it!

Compound Interest at the Dentist's Office

I hope that you understood the power of compound interest from the text explanations, graphs, and tables that I included above, the combination of which is the usual way folks use to teach this concept. But sometimes people need a little extra boost to finally make things click.

I once spent an hour in a youth seminar discussing compound interest, and one student still didn't "get it." I noticed that she had a mouthful of braces just like I did.

(Yes, at the ripe old age of 40-something I'm in braces, AGAIN!) So I pointed out to the class that compounding also works for time, and not just for cash. Here's how. Most folks with braces visit their orthodontist once a month to have the hardware adjusted. This slow and steady approach usually gets your teeth to shift in about 12 to 18 months. I then shared a secret. I was visiting my orthodontist every three weeks, and now I was three months ahead of schedule! By going for adjustments every three weeks, I would receive over the course of a year four extra visits (at no extra charge), and the more rapid pace of adjustments would help my teeth to move more quickly. I was using the compounding principle on time to MY advantage! And I was also saving money!

At this point, my confused student finally "got it!" She knew from her own experience with braces the value of saving time, and she could extrapolate her understanding to money. Now she recognized that saving a little bit of every paycheck would, over time, add up to huge savings.

Give your future self the priceless gift of financial independence. The key is to get started saving today, and to keep saving tomorrow. Give it a try.

Exercise 4: Get enough money to open two savings accounts, one for your long-term needs and one for your short-term big-ticket items and emergencies.

Now, contract with yourself and the Universe to NEVER tap the money in your long-term account until you retire! As the balance of your long-term account grows, check into opening an Individual Retirement Account (IRA) .

Sharing the Wealth: The Giving Branch of the Money Cycle

This topic is my favorite subject when it comes to money, and a lot of my students (of all ages) agree with me. Money likes to flow, and this is the part of the cycle where you help it along. How? By giving money away.

You have certainly heard the proverb that "It is better to give then to receive." Our entire society is based on this idealistic concept. That said, when you practice it with money, it really sinks in. You will actually feel that you are getting far more in return than you ever gave – and you will be right! You do, because the Universe pays you back. An amazing natural law is at work here, but until you try it, you won't totally "get" what I'm talking about.

Spreading the Wealth

I already considered myself a philanthropist when I was only 19 years old. I was majoring in biochemistry (you could tell I was the queen of geeks, couldn't you?) at the University of Missouri, and I was putting myself through school. So, in addition to carrying a full load of classes, I was working three minimum-wage jobs to pay the bills. Despite the stress of living paycheck to paycheck, I already knew just how important it was to harness the Universe's good will on my behalf. I had learned that I needed to give generously if I expected to be rewarded generously. So, every time I got paid I would write my philanthropic checks for $1.37 and send it to my chosen organization.

I still remember a roommate of mine looking at one of my measly checks one day and asking, "Janine, why do you even bother with that? I mean, that amount is hardly worth counting, and after you pay for the stamp, what use is it?" My reply was simple: "Because I want to do what I can. I also know that it will come back to me, somehow." She didn't get it. I considered myself a giver of money; no matter that the amount was paltry. You see, the Universe doesn't care about the amount you give, as long as you have demonstrated that you believe helping people is more important than hoarding cash! Since that long-ago time of poverty, the Universe has gifted me with ample financial resources and numerous giving opportunities. And guess what? I still have a blast writing out checks to organizations that need my help to do good things.

Do you consider yourself a philanthropist? If not, you should. You will need to develop the "giving" mindset to enlist the continuous flow of money through your life. Are you embarrassed that all you can give is 80¢? Don't worry about the amount of money you are sharing. The point is to give. Send it on, and money will flow back to you. Why? Because philanthropic giving primes your monetary pump! By employing the 40/60 Principle to give money away, the Universe can see that you are willing to not only take care of yourself but also to help others in your community who are less fortunate than you. You are showing your maturity with your financial (and spiritual) resources.

Where to Start

When I first mention the principle of philanthropic giving to students, they immediately become overwhelmed by the magnitude of need in our world. Students of all ages come to me regularly suffering from "analysis paralysis" (a condition in which they see so many choices that they are unable to make any choice!) and they beg me for advice. Well, gang, there is a simple way to overcome analysis paralysis. Ready? Here it is. What activities do you like to do? What are you passionate about? Decide what you feel strongly about, and then support institutions that make it happen.

Need some examples? They are all around you. If you are particularly fond of Koala bears in Australia and you want to protect them, give to an organization that does that. Do you want to help homeless people? Then donate to a group that is working on that problem. If everyone on this planet were to give 10% of their income to causes they were personally passionate about, what do you think would happen? That's right. There wouldn't be any suffering. We would wipe it out. So, give to organizations that are doing good works in which you have a personal interest.

My oldest son is 10 years old, and his favorite cause is "The Happy Factory." This organization takes donated lumber and makes wooden toys for kids all over the world who no longer have toys of their own due to the destruction wreaked by natural disasters or wars in their country. It happens that this organization is located in the town where we live. Each year on his birthday, my son visits the building, volunteers some of his time working at the factory (oiling finished toys), and donates the philanthropic 10% of his birthday money. During the year, this organization is "his" philanthropic choice. In fact, he tells me I'm not allowed to contribute to it because he has it covered!

I don't want you to think that once you pick a cause that you have to stick with it from now on. Believe it or not, the Universe will make you aware of other needs in your own community that could use your donations. My husband and I go over our financial records once each year and decide which groups we will continue to support, which ones need to be dropped, and which new ones we will start supporting in the coming year. All the time we are shown new areas where our philanthropic money can have a major impact. The same will happen for you.

Angels on the Street Corner

There is another aspect to philanthropic giving that is hidden from most people. This aspect is the numerous opportunities for unplanned giving that the Universe will throw at you to see if you are paying attention. I have been giving money away for almost 30 years, and I started my streak as an "impulse giver" when I was 12 years old. What do I mean? Well, the usual pattern for me is that I'll be walking down a street, and on the corner will be a guy standing with a sign stating that he needs money so that he can get something to eat. It is so habitual for me to take advantage of these impulsive opportunities that I am reaching for my wallet before I have finished reading the sign. Why? Because I know that the Universe is about to send me money or an opportunity to make money, and I need to prime the pump. This panhandler is actually an angel in disguise, and he is begging on that corner not just to help himself but to help me.

So I walk by the guy and slip a small gift into the bucket – not much, but whatever amount my conscience whispers to me. When I was your age my usual donation was between 25¢ to $2.00, which was all I could afford at the time. I always listen to my conscience when selecting the amount. Within a few days, and sometimes that same day, I will receive a phone call with a job opportunity, or a check will arrive in the mail. Now, you may consider me totally naïve for giving in this fashion. You have probably heard plenty of stories about panhandlers who spend their donations on drugs, or who beg because they make more that way than they could in an "honest" job. You know my response to that? Not ... my ... problem! I am not here as anyone's judge; I am only responsible for giving other people a hand up, in whatever fashion seems best to them. I give my money to them because that is what *I'm* supposed to do. What *they* choose to do with that money once they receive it is so not my issue; it's theirs. I am (and you are) responsible only for listening to what the Universe tells me (and you) to do. Don't look at this person with revulsion! See them for what they are, angels in disguise. The Universe wants to bless you with money, but you must prime the pump first, so dig into your pocket and start giving. Oh, and don't worry about not having any money to give. In over three decades of philanthropy, the Universe has never asked me to donate money I didn't have.

The Universe Gives in Kind, but With Interest

I will tell you a true story regarding the giving of money. I was visiting New Orleans and I happened to walk by a person who was playing the saxophone and had his hat lying on the sidewalk for donations. I listened to his music for a bit and was getting ready to walk away when my conscience whispered to me, "Hey, you need to give this guy three bucks." I quickly opened my wallet and saw that the only bill I had was a $5 bill. I was shocked, because it was the only time in my *life* that I did not have the *exact* amount of change that I thought I should give. I started to fret over this and my conscience added, "Listen, goof ball, just give him the stupid fiver!" So I did. My hotel was three blocks away, and as I walked toward it a small breeze began to blow. I was crossing the street when I was amazed to see a $20 bill rolling toward me. I reached down, picked it up, and started laughing. How crazy is the Universe? I had made a "profit" of 300% in about five minutes! Of course, it doesn't always happen this way, but it has occurred to me often enough that I have learned to listen to my intuition.

Taking Care of Your Second Retirement

Up to now I have focused on philanthropic giving as a means of making the physical world a better place. This is important, but you cannot forget the obligation that you have to share your own ethical and moral values using gifts to a religious institution to help make the emotional and spiritual world a better place as well.

By giving money to your church you are demonstrating to the Universe that you recognize the importance of having a good system of beliefs on which to pattern your life and your relationships with other people. The Universe will reward you to the exact extent that your humanitarian understanding warrants it. Give, and you will get – in this life and the next.

Exercise 5: Pick out a philanthropic organization and a spiritual institution that are in line with your own great purpose. Start aiding their programs by giving them a portion of your money (10% to each). [If you do not belong to an organized religion, then deliver the part you would have given to a church to a philanthropic organization instead.]

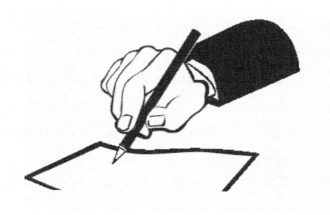

Bringing it all Together

Now for the exciting part. It's time to get money cycling into your life. The advice I gave you in the chapters above will help you figure out the nuts and bolts of making money, and of dividing it into the various pools you will need for it to keep coming your way. Now for the hard part: patience. You must be patient! And yes, I do remember my own young adult years, and I know that patience was not a big part of my life back then. Remember, your financial situation is a marathon and not a sprint. I know that your drive to get as much cash together as soon as you can is huge. You have all sorts of expenses ahead of you. Some of them are quite large and immediate, like a car, college, your own place, running a business, starting a family. I recognize the urgency that you feel at this point in your life. However, I also know that as you continue to use the 40/60 Principle, opportunities for making money and using it wisely will present themselves to you. Over and over. So relax! All the things you want to do will come your way if you continue to implement the 40/60 Principle, track your expenses, and develop a clear purpose to guide your life. And yeah, keep practicing patience.

Your Biggest Test

A warning is in order here. Your confidence *will* be tested! The Universe wants to make sure that you can be trusted with money. Will you wait patiently for the 40/60 Principle to work on your behalf, or will you try to take short cuts to get the things you want? Will you dive into your long-term savings to buy that really sweet skateboard you've been craving, or will you do the right thing and wait until you have earned enough money to buy it using the 40% of your money that makes up your "living" stash? The choice will be up to you. Just keep in mind that once you start abusing the universal laws that govern the flow of money into your life, you will likely continue to do so. And lawbreakers always lose in the end. So stay between the lines when painting your money map.

Another thing to keep in mind is that any time you deal with money you are messing with one of the single most powerful forces in our world. Such power can be used for good or ill. In order to determine your maturity to receive and correctly use more money, the Universe will test you in a variety of ways to make sure that (1) you believe in what you are doing, (2) you are willing to wait on the Universe's timetable and not your own, and (3) you will keep practicing the 40/60 Principle against all financial challenges.

The fact that you will be tested is a tough lesson to hear, and an even tougher one to learn. I prefer that you learn it now because it always easier to form good habits early than it is to break bad ones later. You're young, so you have many years of earning, saving, and giving ahead of you. Take the time now to discover how to manage your money correctly and you'll save yourself loads of stress, heartburn, and pain later. After all, much of the anxiety you see in your parents and other adults is due to everyday financial problems, ones that might not have arisen if they had understood early on how to use money the right way.

You already know how to handle money. You make it, and you spend it. But you have to learn how to use the universal laws of money to your advantage. I have given you these principles in this book. By implementing them, you will be off to a great start in life. However, don't think that you are done once you start experimenting with them. This book is just the beginning of your lifelong financial education. As your money grows and matures, you will need to keep learning what to do with it.

Yep, that's right. The financial strategies that will work for you today as a young adult will need to change and grow as you enter adulthood. So continue studying how best to handle your money. Talk, read, and think. I have given you a short list of resources to study in Appendix 2. Keep your eyes open and you will be able to find lots of additional good resources for yourself. Don't just blindly follow financial advice. You can find a book or website out there to say pretty much anything that you want it to say. So make sure that the things you learn from new sources fit what you have proven for yourself in the past.

In cooking there is an old adage that says "the proof is in the pudding." This saying means that you will be able to see whether or not your recipe was correct by looking at the result. The same proverb holds true for money. When you do something right, you will be rewarded. Screw it up, and you will be disappointed. It's as simple as that.

The Quick Start List to Financial Maturity

Okay, before you put this book down, let's go over a few things you can do right now to get your gravy train started down the tracks.

1. **Break the (Piggy) Bank.** Gather your spare change and split the money in it using the 40/60 Principle.

2. **Plow the Ground.** If you don't have two savings accounts, open them at your local bank. You need a place to plant your seeds. If you don't have enough money to open them now, then get some envelopes and mark them "short-term" and long-term" so you don't get them confused. Open your accounts once your envelopes are bulging!

3. **Catch a Porpoise.** Figure out your purpose in life. What are you passionate about? What do you want to change? How do you wish to impact your world? Answer these questions on a piece of paper. That's right, don't just think about them in the abstract. *You must write them down* if your purpose is to gain any traction in your mind.

4. **Drive on.** After using the 40/60 Principle to allocate your money for three months, read another financial book. Make yourself a promise that you will read a new book on money at least twice a year. (More is definitely better when learning about money!) This

effort will help you become – and stay – financially mature. It is also the only possible way for you to learn enough about money to give yourself the most priceless gift of all: true financial independence.

5. **Branch out.** Don't seek to learn about money just by reading books. The information in older books is often obsolete. Instead, subscribe to magazines and e-zines that discuss money, because the articles in them will keep you up to date on happenings in the financial world and their implications for your personal financial situation.

6. **Stay engaged.** Learn a new skill each month. Keep your mind sharp; a stimulated brain is better able to grasp new concepts, including those that will help you to develop your financial savvy. The best way to hone your mind is to constantly be learning new things. Any kind of thing. The first skill I learned as a 10-year-old just beginning to investigate money was how to cook from scratch. Not only did I become a fantastic chef, but my ability to cook from scratch allowed me to put myself through college both by cooking for other people and by cutting my meal costs by over $3,000 a year. You may learn how to create things (like my main money-making hobbies, crochet and welding) or how to service things (like small engines or appliances). Such skills can give you a solid and fun foundation for your own business or just provide you with a way to make some extra cash on the side after school or while you hold down a full-time job.

7. **Relax!** Breathe! All of this doesn't have to happen in one day! You will have enough money. Just keep living, saving, and giving in the right way (and yep,

that means the 40/60 Principle), and the Universe will make sure that you will have enough money flowing through your life to finish the projects you want to accomplish in this life.

Thank you for buying this book. More importantly, give yourself a pat on the back for taking the initiative to start on your way to financial independence by actually reading it! Do the exercises and follow the principles outlined for you here and you will become a habitual wealth accumulator within three months. I wish you much success in your life.

If you should have any questions for me regarding money, feel free to email me at Janine@smartcentsinc.com. I'll be happy to help you out.

Now, get out that Piggy Bank and get cracking!

Appendix 1:
What if I'm on My Own Already?

First off, congratulations! Heading out on your own is a big step on your road to maturity. But of course, the downside is that you have more expenses. How does your transition to the adult money cycle fit into the equation?

No problem. The universal laws you learned in this book still hold true. The only difference now that you are functioning as an adult is in the way you divide your cash. Adults have more responsibilities, so they get to use more of their incoming money to pay for everyday expenses (like rent!). In short, adults get to split their income according to the 60/40 Principle, like this:

60% for "Living "
20% for "Savings"
    10% for Short-term
    10% for Long-term
20% for "Giving"
    10% for Church
    10% for Philanthropy

The principles for portioning out your life are the same at all ages. Only the amounts are different.

Once you have firmly set your feet on the road to adulthood, you might want to read my financial book for adults, *Money...It's Not Just for Rich People!* This volume discusses ways to cut your expenses while leveraging your money. I go into more detail on how to establish short- and long-term goals and how to decide on a purpose in life.

The Adult Division of Money

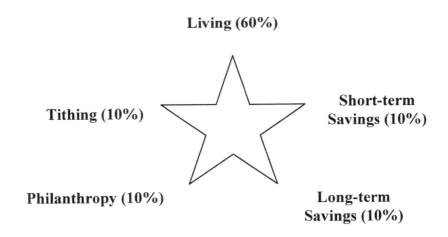

Living (60%)

Tithing (10%)

Short-term
Savings (10%)

Philanthropy (10%)

Long-term
Savings (10%)

Appendix 2: Additional Readings

Okay, now for the bad news. You will have to keep on learning if you want to manage your money rather than having your need for it control you. The good news is that your "homework" will definitely pay off for you (unlike some of those school assignments!).

Before you decide to read any of these books, prove to yourself that the 40/60 Principle really works. You can do that by using the universal laws I have related in this book for at least three months. After that, take a look at this list of advanced resources, see which ones appeal to you, and start reading. And oh yeah, remember to have fun. I know I do when I'm getting ready to get rich....

BOOKS

Aslett, Don; *Clutter's Last Stand* and *Not for Packrats Only;* 1984
The connection between having too much stuff in your life and having bad financial habits is real. When I tell students that part of their money problems stems from having too many things, they look at me like I'm crazy, but it is true. Don Aslett does a brilliant job of teaching you how to keep clutter out of your life, and he does it in such a way that you will actually laugh out loud while reading. You'll also like the line art that he uses to emphasize his points. Keep your living space free of clutter, and watch money and stuff you really want start to flow into your life.

Bach, David; *The Automatic Millionaire*; 2004

Bach is a professional financial planner. In this book he tells the story of an unassuming couple that came to him for advice on financial independence. Instead they ended up *teaching him* how to become wealthy. This book is a fast read and gives many great pointers on how to make your wealth accumulation program automatic. I recommend this book to my students who have a steady paycheck. As Bach says, make your savings automatic and your ability to grow your wealth is assured!

Bolon, Janine; *Money ... It's Not Just for Rich People*; 2005

Yep, this is a totally shameless recommendation of my own book on the subject of wealth accumulation and financial independence. On the other hand, this volume is filled with tools that really work, tools that you will need to change your attitude and habits about money and confront the main mental obstacles you harbor that might keep you from becoming wealthy. I give you simple systems and exercises to allow you to start doing small things each week that will rapidly move you from a mentality of poverty to a mindset of abundance.

Dacyczyn, Amy; *The Tightwad Gazette* (three volumes); 1995

I recommend that anybody who wants to truly learn the fine art of frugality read this book, even if you already think that you're frugal. Better yet, buy this book so that you always have it near you as a source of new tips. Amy Dacyczyn (pronounced "decision") is incredible when it comes to saving money. I guarantee that you will learn something. I still reread it from cover to cover every year, and I refer to it on a monthly basis!

Long, Charles; *How to Live Without a Salary*; 1980

I enjoy Long's laid-back view on life and his ability to leverage his money by haggling. I learned the art of barter through this book and how to think through what I thought I needed versus what I really needed. He is an excellent resource to teach you alternative ways of getting what you want out of life without having to spend a dime. That's a good habit to develop when you don't have a lot of money in hand. You know, like if you're an unemployed young adult.

Stanley, Thomas & Danko, William; *The Millionaire Next Door*; 1996

You'll find out how *real* millionaires live in this book, not the so-rich-they-burn-money caricatures that you find in Hollywood productions. The research Stanley and Danko have done is eye-opening and mind-blowing. They asked 385 real but "ordinary" millionaires about their lifestyles, how they spend their money, and what they really like to do for leisure. If you aspire to financial maturity now and real financial independence later, this book will give you a great roadmap for the habits of successful wealth accumulators.

MAGAZINES

Bottom Line / Personal. This bimonthly publication is a good way to start learning about how money (and the need for it) can impact your life. Each issue includes practical discussions and brief tips about good financial investments for today, opportunities to purchase high-quality items at cheaper prices, and advice for living a healthier and more fulfilled life (which indirectly will save you loads of money in the future!). The first six issues are free!

www.bottomlinesecrets.com

Money, This monthly magazine is my favorite overall way for learning how to handle money. Topics in every issue include financial trends, options for personal financial growth, and recommendations for various consumer items (such as cars, computers, and digital cameras) that are the "best values" for your money. I highly recommend this magazine to get you started in thinking about how to work with your money as an up-and-coming adult.

money.cnn.com/magazines/moneymag

Smart Money. This monthly magazine is published by the Wall Street Journal and has specialists in money discuss the latest trends on how best to make your money grow. This is a good magazine to get when you start learning how to manage your own investment accounts.

www.smartmoney.com

Young Money. This magazine, published six times a year, contains stories relevant to the needs and lifestyles of young adult and college students. I don't receive this periodical (since my fiscal needs are different), but you might want to check it out. Just compare the advice given in the magazine to the universal laws I have given you in this book.

www.youngmoney.com

E-ZINES

The Dollar Stretcher. Gary Foreman, a retired financial planner, started this free e-zine when he was laid off from his last job. He sends it out weekly, and you can go to his web site for additional articles and advice. I've spoken with Mr. Foreman on the telephone many times, and he has a special interest in helping youth get out and stay out of debt (particularly of the credit card variety). Give his site a well-deserved look.

www.stretcher.com

Living on a Dime, This free e-zine is dedicated to the ideal of living frugally. It was started by Tawra Jean Kellam and her mom, Jill Cooper. They have also written a great book on how to live cheaply (called *Not Just Beans: 50 Years of Frugal Family Favorites*). I have spoken with Tawra on the telephone, and I find her energy and enthusiasm to be contagious. You can learn more about Tawra and Jill's stories on their site:

www.livingonadime.com

WEBSITES

There are literally thousands of websites that can help you learn more about handling your money. The list below comprises the sites that I use most frequently, so I know from experience that they will make a good starting place for you.

www.cheapskatemonthly.com
Mary Hunt started this website after writing her book, *The Complete Cheapskate*. In it she tells her story of having accumulated thousands of dollars in credit card debt as well as the steps she took to dig out after 14 years. She provides lots of tips and thoughts on money that will help you on your own financial path.

www.fidelity.com
This site by Fidelity Investments is one of many offerings presented by large mutual fund companies. It includes lots of information to help novice investors become savvy wealth accumulators by discussing current financial trends and also by describing how good investors manage their assets. Contact them to learn more about their youth-specific programs for your age group. I have found their customer service representatives to be courteous and delightfully patient when answering my many questions!

www.finishrich.com

This gem is David Bach's website. Yep, the same guy who authored one of the books I recommended in my list above (*The Automatic Millionaire*). David's big focus now is how to become wealthy using real estate, but look at his earlier works published in book form and his advice is perfect for young people learning to save and live on modest incomes.

www.vanguard.com

Vanguard is another mutual fund company with a website designed to both educate and empower individual investors. I find their representatives to be just as helpful as the folks at Fidelity. Don't get overwhelmed by all the options given on the site and just give up. Contact them; that's what they are there for. It is in their best interest that you know what you are doing!

These following web sites are some of my favorite ones dedicated to "general purpose" financial education. Articles cover financial matters in the United States and throughout the world. Common topics are current market conditions, predicted financial trends, proposed legislation and policies that might affect your money, and the biographies and paths to success of entrepreneurs (including many young people).

AOL:	**money.aol.com/**
CNN:	**http://money.cnn.com/**
Motley Fool:	**www.fool.com/**
Yahoo:	**finance.yahoo.com/**

Notes

(Here are a few extra pages where you can put your notes!)

CPSIA information can be obtained
at www.ICGtesting.com
Printed in the USA
BVOW03s2306151217
502935BV00001B/101/P